I LIKE SCHOOL

Written by
Sarah Toast

Cover illustrated by
Eddie Young

Interior illustrated by
Steve Henry

Louis Weber, C.E.O.
Publications International, Ltd.
7373 North Cicero Avenue
Lincolnwood, Illinois 60646

Permission is never granted for commercial purposes.

Manufactured in U.S.A.

8 7 6 5 4 3 2 1

ISBN: 0-7853-1071-1

PUBLICATIONS INTERNATIONAL, LTD.
Little Rainbow is a trademark of Publications International, Ltd.

This is Jake's first day of school. He feels happy and scared at the same time. He's happy because he knows he'll see his friends and he has heard school is fun. But he's scared because he doesn't know his teacher and he might miss his mom.

His mom takes him to the classroom and says hello to Jake's teacher, Miss Martin. Miss Martin is nice. She even says hello to Jake's stuffed dog Snarf. Snarf has come along to keep Jake company this first day of school.

Jake kisses his mom good-bye and takes a look around the classroom. It looks like a pretty interesting place.

"Jake, why don't you find the cubby with your name on it. You can put your backpack in there. You may even find a little surprise," says Miss Martin.

Jake's welcome-to-school surprise is
an eraser shaped like a funny dinosaur.
"Thank you, Miss Martin," says Jake.

When everyone has arrived, Miss Martin says, "Please sit in a chair at one of the tables." The chairs and tables are just the right size for children.

Jake says hello to three of his pals.

He doesn't know the rest of the children.

Miss Martin asks them to say their names

for the rest of the class.

Everyone gets a classroom job to do for a week. This week Jake will feed the fish with his friend Mark. Mark has a fish at home. He says, "You can feed the fish first, Jake. I do it all the time."

Mark shows Jake how much food to sprinkle into the water. "It isn't good to feed fish too much food. It could make them sick," says Mark.

Some more of the classroom jobs are to water the plants and straighten the books on the bookshelves. Some children hand out papers, crayons, and scissors. Others help Miss Martin decorate a bulletin board with leaves made out of construction paper.

When all the classroom jobs are finished, Miss Martin says, "Line up! It is time for recess." She leads the class to the playground right outside the school.

First Jake plays in the sandbox with a boy and girl he has just met. Then he takes a turn on the swings with his friend from across the street.

Miss Martin calls for everyone to line up again when recess is over. She leads the class back to the room and says, "It is time for a snack. Please find your seat."

Jake is hungry! Some helpers pass out cookies, fruit, and little cartons of cold milk. The boys and girls get to know each other while they eat their snacks.

After snacks Miss Martin asks the class to join her in the art corner for finger painting. Mrs. Wiggins is the art teacher. She tells everyone to be creative.

Jake spreads paint on wet paper with his hands and makes squiggles with his fingers. It feels squishy and slippery.

"Nice job, Jake," says Miss Martin.

The children hang their paintings to dry. Then everyone washes their hands and hangs up their smocks to dry, too. Miss Martin asks, "Who would like to hear a good story?"

The children raise their hands and say, "We do!" Everyone follows Miss Martin to the story rug. This is a time to get comfortable and listen quietly while Miss Martin reads. Some children go to the play area to find a stuffed toy to cuddle with. Jake brings Snarf to the story rug.

Today's story is about a tugboat and a steamship. Miss Martin never forgets to show the pictures.

When the story is finished, Miss Martin says, "Your first day of school is over. Your mothers and fathers are outside."

Jake's mother is waiting for him. Jake runs to her and says, "I have a surprise for you, Mom! I made it in school."

Jake's mother tapes her wonderful
surprise onto the refrigerator door.
"I like this sun," she says.

"And I like school," says Jake.